Bantam Books in the Choose Your Own Adventure® Series
Ask your bookseller for the books you have missed

SECRET OF THE SUN GOD

BY ANDREA PACKARD

ILLUSTRATED BY YEE CHEA LIN

An Edward Packard Book

BANTAM BOOKS
TORONTO • NEW YORK • LONDON • SYDNEY • AUCKLAND

RL 4, IL age 10 and up

SECRET OF THE SUN GOD
A Bantam Book / June 1987

CHOOSE YOUR OWN ADVENTURE® *is a registered trademark of
Bantam Books, Inc. Registered in U.S. Patent and Trademark
Office and elsewhere.
Original conception of Edward Packard.*

ISBN 0-553-26529-6

Published simultaneously in the United States and Canada

PRINTED IN THE UNITED STATES OF AMERICA

O   0 9 8 7 6 5 4 3 2 1

To Kate Watkins and Lisa Gillim,
Erika Bass and Beverly Harding

WARNING!!!

Do not read this book straight through from beginning to end. These pages contain many different adventures you may have when you search for the Olmetecan Temple of the Sun in Mexico. From time to time as you read along, you will be asked to make decisions and choices. Your choices may lead to success or disaster.

The adventures you have will be the result of your own choices. After you make a choice, follow the instructions to see what happens to you next.

Beware! The secret of the Sun God can bring danger as well as great luck.

Have fun!

This is the summer you've been waiting for! Your aunt Eloisa has promised that you can join her archaeological expedition in Mexico. She's been searching for the Olmetecan Temple of the Sun. Now, with your vacation just two weeks away, Eloisa is calling to tell you about the lost Temple.

"Five hundred years ago the Olmetecans were a great nation," Eloisa tells you. "They built huge pyramids to Omoteo, their Sun God, and understood the movements of the stars better than any nation of that time. They had shaman-leaders, great priests who saw the will of their Sun God in all of nature. When the Spanish invaded Mexico in 1521, most of the Olmetecans died fighting the Spanish soldiers. But some of them fled to the mountains in the south."

Turn to page 2.

"What happened to them there?" you ask.

"People say that when the Olmetecans reached the mountains, they built a temple to the Sun God and buried their sacred treasures there. Then their shaman prayed to the Sun God for the power to protect his people forever from invaders. Legend says that the Sun God gave the shaman the power to start and stop earthquakes. Today, when companies try to mine the silver in these mountains, earthquakes stop them from cutting down the forests. Some believe the Olmetecans still live hidden in those mountains and start the earthquakes to protect their sacred land. To this day, though, the Olmetecans and the Temple have never been found.

"But finally I've found a clue in a tiny Mexican village called Cholula. We'll start our expedition from there. If we find the Temple of the Sun, maybe we can discover the fate of the Olmetecan nation!"

Turn to page 4.

Several days later the President of Mexico gives you and Eloisa national medals of honor for capturing the most wanted smugglers in the nation. "Our entire police force failed to stop these men!" he says.

You smile and nod, but secretly you're wondering about the eagle. Was it protecting you and Eloisa? Was it guarding the Temple? One thing is certain—Eagle Mountain still holds many mysteries.

The End

4

The last days of school before your vacation seem to last forever. Finally, just as you're leaving for the airport, a package arrives for you from Mexico. It's from Eloisa. Inside the package you find a beautiful poncho. On one side is a mountain shaped like an eagle beneath a huge sun. A mazelike pattern covers the other side. When you look closely at the faded pattern, you see what look like strange animals drawn with circles, squiggles, and squares. Eloisa's letter is even more surprising.

This poncho is the clue I've been looking for! A native of these mountains named Orlando gave it to me. He says it's an Olmetecan cloak of protection. I haven't had time to study it, but the sun-eagle pattern looks like a landmark near the village of Cholula: Eagle Mountain. The Temple could be there!

The bad news is that two men think I've already found the Temple. They've tried to make me take them there. They don't care about the Temple. They just want to steal its treasures. I'm sending you the poncho to keep it out of their hands. When you fly to Mexico, wear the poncho inside out to hide the eagle-mountain pattern. See you at the airport!

Love, Eloisa

P.S. If something goes wrong, find Orlando!

Turn to page 7.

When you wake you're lying on a soft bed in a sunny room. Eloisa is sitting by your side! Both her arms are in casts, but she's smiling. "What happened?" you ask.

"You fainted," Eloisa says.

"I mean what happened to *you*?" you say. Eloisa looks down at her two casts. "The smugglers forced me to lead them to Eagle Mountain," she says. "But when I said I didn't know where the Temple is, they didn't believe me. The villagers came just in time."

"How'd you get hurt?" you ask.

"When the villagers came, the smugglers started shooting at them," Eloisa says. "I broke away and dove to the ground—and the ground was pretty hard."

Eloisa laughs and taps her casts together. "It'll be a long time before I can do any exploring again," she says. "But thanks to you, we're both safe. And when we search for the Temple again, those men will be safe too—safe behind bars!"

The End

As you put on the poncho inside out, you wonder about the men looking for the Temple. Have they threatened Eloisa? Is she in danger? You are still wondering about these questions a few hours later as your plane descends over the mountains of southwest Mexico.

You step down from the plane with your knapsack and head toward the gate to find Eloisa. But she's nowhere in sight. After half an hour you go to the information desk. "Can you help me call my aunt in Cholula?" you ask.

"I'm sorry," the woman answers. "Cholula is a tiny village in the mountains—it still doesn't have any phone service."

"Then how can I get there?" you ask.

"It's a long way—a five-hour bus trip," the woman says. "The next bus leaves for Cholula in a couple of hours."

Go on to the next page.

Two hours later, when Eloisa still hasn't arrived, you board a rickety old bus to Cholula. A young woman sits next to you holding a live chicken firmly in her lap. More people crowd onto the bus until the aisle is completely jammed. The bus starts up with a rumble and lurches along the rutted roads.

As you drive farther from the airport, pas-

sengers get off the crowded bus and you see fewer
and fewer houses. Sometimes the bus stops far
from any village. The woman next to you gets off
in what looks like the middle of nowhere.

Go on to the next page.

By late afternoon, the bus has climbed high into the mountains, and you're the only passenger left. Finally the bus stops at the edge of a tiny village where houses made of adobe and wooden boards are scattered on a hill rising up from the bank of a river.

"Last stop, Cholula," the driver tells you. You step down from the bus and stand in the dusty road. No one is in sight.

You had hoped that Eloisa might meet you here at the edge of town. But you can't see her anywhere!

As the bus pulls away, you start up a dirt path that leads between a cluster of adobe houses. What's happened to Eloisa? You want to find her as soon as possible. On the other hand, if something's gone wrong, maybe you should try to find Orlando first—whoever he is.

If you try to find Orlando, turn to page 14.

If you try to find Eloisa's house first, turn to page 17.

You hurry out of Eloisa's house and look up and down the dirt path. Just up the path, you see two men leaning on a fence. You run to them for help.

"My aunt Eloisa's house has been ransacked and I can't find her anywhere!" you say.

"This is terrible!" the tall man says, stroking his mustache. "But I can help you, I'm Eloisa's friend. My name is Juan, and this is my friend Ramon. We're the only policemen in Cholula."

"Come with us," Ramon says. "We'll see what we can do."

You sigh with relief as Juan and Ramon lead you to an adobe house by the woods. Once you're inside, Juan offers you a chair.

"Your aunt has stirred up a lot of trouble," he tells you. "People say she's found a map to the Temple of the Sun. Whoever ransacked her house must be looking for Eloisa's map. She went into hiding two days ago. Maybe she sent you the map to keep it safe."

Ramon leans toward you across the table. His breath smells of stale cigar smoke. "Tell us what your aunt sent you! Her life and the safety of the treasure depend upon it!"

You're not sure you should tell Juan and Ramon about the poncho.

If you tell Ramon about the poncho Eloisa sent you, turn to page 19.

If you say you don't know anything about the Temple, turn to page 20.

"Please, just trust me!" Diego answers. "The men could be on our trail right now. Did anyone see you get off the bus? Was anyone following us?"

"No, you're the first person I've met here," you say. "Why should anyone follow *us*?"

Diego turns to you. "Because there are two men who've been watching Eloisa's house. Eloisa says they lead a smuggling ring that steals treasures from museums. They want her to take them to the Temple of the Sun so they can steal its treasures. That's why Eloisa's hiding. But if they can't find her, they'll come after *you*!"

Diego glances out of the window and then clenches his fists. He runs to the window and pulls the curtain over it.

"Two men are coming up the hill!" Diego says. "You've got to hide!" You run to a closet and open the door, but the closet is small and bare.

Suddenly the door bursts open. Two men stride into the room. They point their guns at you. "One word and I'll shoot!" the tall man snaps.

"We've caught two birds in one nest," he says, turning to Diego. "Your godfather has unlucky friends. So do you. We'll have to clip your wings."

The fat man grabs Diego and ties him to a chair. "By the time your friends find you we'll be long gone," the tall man tells Diego.

"Who are you?" you ask the man.

"Shut up!" he orders. "Or we'll shut you up for good!" He laughs, puts his gun to your back, and pushes you out of the house.

Turn to page 67.

You look up at the many houses clustered on the hillside, wondering which one is Orlando's. Then you see a boy carrying pails of water.

"Hello, there," you call, walking toward him. "Do you know where Orlando lives? My aunt didn't meet me at the airport, and she told me to find Orlando if something happened to her."

The boy stops short, puts down his buckets, and stares at you. "Is Eloisa your aunt?" he whispers.

You nod.

"Orlando's my godfather," he whispers. "My name is Diego. Please come to my house. It's not safe for you here in the street."

Diego carries your knapsack for you and leads you to a small adobe house by the edge of the forest. Once you're inside, he closes the door and turns to you. "You were right to look for Orlando," he says. "Eloisa is hiding out in his cabin in the woods. She's waiting for you there."

"Hiding? What's the matter?" you ask.

"There's no time to explain," Diego says. "There's a path behind the house. Follow it to a river and then go upstream to a waterfall. There you'll find a path that leads to Orlando's cabin." Diego glances out the window. "Please hurry," he says, "They may come looking for you here!"

Who is Eloisa hiding from? You feel you can trust Diego, but you hesitate to leave without knowing what's happened.

If you say you have to know more before you go, turn to page 12.

If you go now to Orlando's cabin, turn to page 18.

The fire burns out as quickly as it flared. Suddenly, a heavy hand grips your shoulder. It's Oloac! He's standing right by your side.

"You have shown you are friends of the Olmeteca," Oloac says. "Your offering means more than if you'd never trespassed on this sacred ground."

"We saw your face in the flames!" you say. "Did you start the fire? What happened here?"

"This is just one of the secrets of the Sun God." Oloac says. "The greatest mysteries and medicine powers can not be stolen or told in a word. But if you will come back to our village, they will be yours to learn and share with us."

As you and Eloisa follow Tomi and Oloac back to the Olmetecan village, the setting sun is casting purple ribbons of light across the clouds. It's the end of a long day, but your adventure is just beginning.

The End

You continue up the dirt path until you come to a small wooden house. A boy near the front gate is putting a saddle on a donkey. His dark eyes stare at you over the donkey's back. "Hello," you call. "Can you tell me where Eloisa lives?"

"Sure," the boy answers. "Just follow this path. It's after the schoolhouse on your right. There's a big garden out front."

"Thanks," you say, heading up the hill. Soon you pass the school and walk through Eloisa's garden to the front door.

"Hello, I'm here!" you call, stepping through the open kitchen doorway.

The sight before you stops you short. Eloisa's house has been ransacked!

Your heart pounds as you walk through the kitchen and look into the bedroom. The mirrors are smashed. Broken glass is scattered everywhere. Someone has slashed the mattress and pinned a note to the torn stuffing.

ELOISA: THIS IS YOUR FINAL WARNING. LEAD US TO THE TEMPLE OF THE SUN OR THIS WILL BE YOUR LAST EXPEDITION!

Who would want to hurt Eloisa? Where is she? You've got to get help. Eloisa told you to find Orlando if something happened. But did she expect something as serious as this? Maybe you should go to the police first.

If you go to the police first, turn to page 11.

If you try to find Orlando, turn to page 22.

"I'll go to the cabin," you tell Diego.

Diego claps you on the back. "Good luck," he says.

You hurry through Orlando's backyard and find the path through the woods. The trees are full of dark, shifting shadows. You can't help glancing behind you to make sure that no one is following you.

You clamber over several ridges until you reach the stream Diego told you about. Finally you climb up the steep rocks near a waterfall and turn down a narrow path that leads away from the stream.

It's getting so dark that you almost walk past the tiny cabin hidden in a dense grove of pine and oak.

Turn to page 21.

You take off the poncho and spread it on the table. "Eloisa sent me this," you tell the men. "She told me to keep the pattern hidden."

Spread out, the pattern looks like a map. "This is it!" Ramon cries. "The eagle—it looks like Eagle Mountain! We're sure to find the treasure there!"

"You fool!" Juan shouts at Ramon. "You always blow our cover! Now what are we going to do with the kid?"

Horrified, you start to run for the door. But Juan beats you there. He grabs your arms and twists them behind your back. "Gag this brat!" he orders Ramon. Ramon stuffs a dirty rag into your mouth.

"Don't worry, Juan," he says. "I didn't blow it. This map tells us to go to Eagle Mountain, but from there we need the kid to lead us to the Temple."

"But I don't know where it is!" you say.

"You can't fool us," says Ramon. "Even if you didn't know how to find the Temple, we wouldn't leave you behind to help the cops find *us.*"

"Let's get going while there's still light," Juan says, grabbing your poncho. Ramon shoves you out the back door and into a jeep.

The road is so overgrown with brush that it's already dusk by the time you reach the base of Eagle Mountain. The barren peak is shaped like the head of an eagle. On your left, the east face slopes down like a great wing stretching out toward the horizon.

Juan pulls the rag out of your mouth. "Scream all you want now," he says. "There's no one for miles to hear you."

Turn to page 25.

You decide not to trust Juan and Ramon. You're glad you wore the poncho inside out to hide the pattern. "Eloisa didn't tell me how to find the Temple," you say. "Well, I've got to go now."

"You'll stay right here!" Juan snaps. "We'll need you for further questioning."

You start toward the door, but Ramon grabs your arm. "It's for your own protection," he growls. Ramon shoves you into a small back room, grabs your knapsack, and locks the door.

Now you know for sure that Juan and Ramon are lying. They must be the ones who ransacked Eloisa's house.

Through the thin wall you can hear them talking. "Now what'll we do with the kid?" Ramon says. "There's nothing in this knapsack."

"We'll get what we want," Juan says. "Eloisa escaped—but we'll make the kid talk."

Will they search you next—or worse? You look around the room for a way out. You try to open the shutters, but they're nailed shut. In one corner is a footstool. Maybe you could use it to break the shutters and escape through the window. But, if Juan and Ramon catch you, there's no telling what they might do to you.

Your other thought is to pretend you know how to find the Temple. Then you might find a better chance to escape.

If you try to break open the shutters and escape, turn to page 60.

If you pretend to know how to find the Temple, turn to page 41.

You walk up to the cabin as a short woman with curly gray hair steps out onto the porch. It's Eloisa!

"Come in! I'm so glad you're safe!" she says. "I didn't think I'd have to hide out here, but these men are more dangerous than I realized."

"Who are they?" you ask. "Why must you hide?"

"They're leaders of a smuggling ring," Eloisa says. "They don't care about the Olmetecans—they just want to steal the Temple's treasures. If they find me, they'll try to make me lead them to the Temple of the Sun—and I haven't even found it yet. My only clue is the poncho I sent you."

"Do you know anything else about the poncho?" you ask.

"Only that it's an Olmetecan cloak of protection," Eloisa answers. "Orlando said I should never go to Eagle Mountain without it."

"Couldn't Orlando tell you more?" you ask.

"He knows many secrets about Eagle Mountain, but he says he's waiting for the right time to share them. He'll be back any day from a trip to gather herbs from the forest, but now that these smugglers want to loot the Temple, I can't wait. I've got to start searching the mountain."

You want to explore Eagle Mountain too. On the other hand, there may be good reasons why no one goes there. Perhaps you should first wait for Orlando and ask him what he knows.

If you say you'll go to Eagle Mountain with Eloisa, turn to page 30.

If you wait to hear what Orlando has to say first, turn to page 37.

You start to walk out of Eloisa's house, wondering how you'll find Orlando. Then you notice the corner of an envelope poking out from a pile of spilled flour and broken jars.

Did Eloisa leave you a note? You pick up the envelope, open it, and read the scrawled message inside.

Eloisa,
  I'm sorry to hear of your danger.
  I hope you'll stay in my cabin until it's safe again. Here's a map showing the way to my cabin. Make sure no one follows you!
                                              —Orlando

You slip out the back door and hurry toward the edge of the woods. If men are watching Eloisa's house you don't want them to follow you either. You walk into the dense brush, waiting until the village is well out of sight before you stop to look at the map.

Suddenly you hear a twig snap just a few yards away. You swing around and look. A tall man with a huge mustache is spying on you from behind a tree—and he knows you've seen him! The man darts around the tree. He's coming toward you!

Turn to page 112.

Carefully you lower yourself down from the doorway toward the narrow ledge. Your heart is pounding as you search for each foothold.

It seems to take forever to reach the ledge. *Have you reached it?* The ledge is barely the width of your foot. But there's no turning back. You cling to the rock face with both hands as you inch sideways toward the gentle slope.

Just as you reach the slope you hear shouts from the cabin. "The kid's escaped—or fallen!"

They know you're gone! Will they start searching for you? You don't wait to find out. You scramble up the slope, hurry over the ridge, and run down a hill into the valley below. You run as far as you can into the forest. You stop by a huge tree.

Now that you've escaped from the cabin, how will you get back to Cholula? You've run so far into the woods that you're not even sure how to get back to the cabin.

You wander over the rocky terrain and climb a high ridge covered with juniper trees. Maybe you can spot a house or a village from higher ground. But the mountains and valleys below look wild and unfamiliar. As the sun starts to set, the shadows grow longer and darker around you. Soon it will be harder than ever to find your way.

Suddenly a twig snaps behind you. You swing around, hardly daring to breathe as you search the shadows. Have your kidnappers tracked you?

Silently an Indian boy steps from behind a tree. He places an arrow in his bow, shoots it at the setting sun, and steps toward you.

Turn to page 34.

Ramon builds a fire and heats up a can of chili. The food tastes like old tin cans, but you're hungry. You gulp down your tiny share. After dinner Juan ties your hands behind your back. "You'll sleep tight tonight!" He laughs, then adds, "Tomorrow we look for the treasure." He puts the poncho on you and spreads out blankets for Ramon and himself. In a few minutes they're snoring loudly.

But you can't sleep. You struggle to wrench free of your bonds, but Juan has made the knots tight. What will you do in the morning when they tell you to lead them to the Temple? You sit staring out into the darkness for hours.

Then, in the distance, you see a faint light. It looks like a bonfire high up on the east face of Eagle Mountain. Perhaps there are people there who can help you. But the light seems to be pretty high up on the mountain. You could easily walk away without waking Juan and Ramon, but do you dare try to climb the mountain at night with your hands tied behind you?

Your other thought is to wait until morning and try to lead Juan and Ramon to where the light is now shining. Whoever lit the fire might still be there to help you.

If you try to climb up to the bonfire now, turn to page 52.

If you wait until morning, then lead Juan and Ramon to where the fire is burning, turn to page 32.

A few minutes later the two men open the door. "Your time's up," the tall man says. "Where is she?"

You can only hope you'll both find a safer way to escape later. "Eloisa's hiding in Orlando's cabin," you say.

"Curse it! Why didn't you think of it?" the tall man tells his partner. Then he turns to you. "She'd better be there," he says, "or you'll pay for it!"

The men push you into the jeep and drive to the edge of Cholula, where they hide the jeep in a thicket and search the woods behind Diego's house.

"I know it's here somewhere," the fat man says. By now the sun is setting and the woods are growing dark. The tall man holds you by the arm—and his grip grows tighter every minute.

Finally you stumble on the tiny shack nestled in a grove of trees. "This is it!" the fat man says, drawing his gun. He goes to the door and breaks it down.

A gray-haired woman leaps to her feet. It's Eloisa! Before you can call to her, the tall man puts his gun to your head. "Lead us to the Temple or I'll shoot!" he shouts.

Eloisa turns white as a sheet. "I—I'll take you there," she says. "But it's dark. I can't find it at night."

The tall man frowns. "Then we'll leave at dawn," he says. "Until then, you're not going anywhere!"

Go on to the next page.

The two men tie you and Eloisa to a large loom standing in one corner of the cabin. They lie down on blankets near the wood stove, and soon they're snoring like bulldozers.

You struggle for hours to loosen the cords binding your wrists. "I can't get loose," Eloisa whispers, "Can you?"

"Maybe," you say. Your wrists are burning from rubbing against the cords. At last you pull your hands and legs free. But the sky is already growing light.

"There's no time to untie me," Eloisa says. "Run to Cholula and get help!"

You struggle to your feet and inch toward the door. The two men are still snoring. Then you notice a gun lying under the fat man's pillow. Could you grab it without waking him?

If you run to Cholula for help, turn to page 39.

If you try to get the fat man's gun,
turn to page 42.

You start up the slope on your left and slowly try to retrace your steps to Cholula. But after a few minutes you begin to think you've lost your own trail. None of the trees and rocks look familiar. You walk farther on and then turn back toward the stream. At least you can still try the other direction. But in the fading light the woods are becoming dark with shadows. You walk for a long time without reaching the river. You're lost!

You huddle all night at the base of a huge tree. When the sun finally rises you haven't slept at all. You start searching again, but you find no signs of Cholula or any other village. Even the stream is nowhere to be found.

The next night you manage to sleep, but you wake up feeling too weak to go on. Then, through the branches to your left, you notice a movement. It's smoke rising!

You struggle to your feet and stagger toward the smoke. After a few minutes, you reach a small clearing where thatched huts are clustered on a gentle slope. The smell of cooking fires makes you hungrier than ever. You begin to feel faint.

Just ahead, several women are building a fire. They have long black braids and wear beaded skirts. "Hello . . . Help!" you cry hoarsely. You're so thirsty you can barely speak.

The women turn toward you in surprise. You start toward them. Suddenly the ground tilts sharply up before you. You close your eyes as a wave of darkness rushes over you.

Turn to page 65.

"Wonderful!" Eloisa cries, jumping to her feet, when you agree to go with her. "Let's pack our knapsacks tonight and get an early start tomorrow morning."

The next morning you put on your poncho with the right side out. "If this is an Olmetecan cloak of protection, I guess I'll wear the right side out when we go to Eagle Mountain," you say.

"Well, there's no need to hide the pattern now," Eloisa says. "Even if the smugglers track us to the mountain, the pattern won't tell them anything more about how to find the Temple."

You hike all morning with Eloisa until you reach the top of a high ridge. Across a green valley you see a huge mountain whose rocky summit rises up like the head of an eagle. "It must be Eagle Mountain!" you say.

Looking due north from where you stand, you can see both the east and west faces. Eloisa scans the mountain with her binoculars. "It looks as though the east face is full of caves," she says. "Some Indian nations have built huge cities of cliff dwellings. Perhaps the Temple is there."

The west face of the mountain slopes down from the summit in the shape of a great wing. "There's a mesa on the western face. The Temple could also be there. Which side of the mountain do you want to explore first?" Eloisa asks you.

If you say you want to explore the caves on the east face, turn to page 44.

If you say you want to explore the western mesa, turn to page 48.

"I'll go with you," you tell Tomi. This may be a chance you'll never have again.

Tomi sets a fast pace through the woods. When you finally reach Eagle Mountain, he leads you up a rocky slope. "The secret passage is just ahead," Tomi says.

Suddenly you hear a sharp cry up ahead. Stones clatter down the slope. "Someone's up there!" you say. You scramble up the slope as fast as you can. "Hello!" you call. "Is anyone there?" In front of you is a deep crevice in the slope. You edge toward the crevice and look down.

"Help!" a faint voice calls from below. It's Eloisa!

"Thank heavens you're here," she cries. "I was searching for the Temple, but I've fallen and jammed my foot between two rocks. I'm trapped!"

You and Tomi scramble down to her. Then you both pull away loose stones, lift the rock trapping Eloisa's foot, and help her out of the crevice.

As you tell Eloisa what happened to you, her face brightens. "I never dreamed the Olmeteca still live in these mountains," she tells Tomi, "and now you've both saved my life! How can I ever thank you?"

Tomi turns to you. "I might have led us into this very trap," he says. "We must thank the Sun God that we saved your aunt from it instead."

Turn to page 95.

32

It would be risky enough to climb Eagle Mountain at night. You don't dare try it with your hands tied behind you. You stare all night at the bonfire burning high up on Eagle Mountain. Finally, just as you're falling asleep, Juan wakes you.

"Let's go!" he says, untying your hands. "And I'm warning you: If you give us a false lead, we'll bury you in the first empty hole we dig!"

You lead the way up the rocky mountain slope. Ramon carries a shovel on his shoulder. Juan keeps his gun drawn and ready.

Finally you reach the high plateau. In a clearing near the edge of the cliff, you find the ashes of the bonfire. No one is in sight. What will you do now?

Juan's face is as red as a rotten tomato. Ramon kicks at the pile of charred logs. "Someone's been here before us!" he cries. Just beyond the ashes he finds a huge mound of newly turned earth. "And someone's been digging!" he says.

"No!" Juan shouts. "I won't have the treasure taken from under my nose!" Juan waves his gun at you. "Dig!" he orders. "And don't stop until you find the treasure!"

"Juan, are you crazy?" Ramon says. "The Temple can't be under this new mound of earth."

"Shut up!" Juan shouts. "Let the kid dig!"

You dig long into the hot afternoon. Your hands become so blistered you can hardly hold the shovel. Just as you feel you can dig no longer, you turn up a thick layer of ashes.

Scattered among the ashes are white chips. They're pieces of bone!

Turn to page 103.

You step through the thicket and walk toward the fire. You kneel on the ground like the Olmetecans and bow your head forward.

The Olmetecans look at you as if you're a ghost. They stand up, but don't move. Then the bleeding woman walks slowly toward you. She stares at your poncho, then into your eyes, her own eyes full of questions. You lean over so that the woman can see your tied hands. Quickly she cuts the rope with her knife. You nod and smile your thanks.

"Olmetecans?" you ask, pointing to the people behind her. The woman answers you rapidly in a strange language. When she sees that you don't understand, she points to your poncho and then to herself. Tears well up in her eyes.

If your poncho is Olmetecan, what does it mean to her? Not knowing what else to do, you take it off and give it to the woman. Her face brightens, and she smiles through her tears. Then she puts on the poncho and points to herself. "Katai," she says.

Katai turns and speaks to the other Olmetecans. At her words, they start to leave the clearing. Katai stays with you as they disappear into the brush.

Katai opens a pouch on her belt and takes out a silver amulet on a leather cord. She rubs the amulet between her fingers and cups her hand to her ear as if listening to a faint sound. Then she puts the amulet in your hand and holds your hand to your ear. What is she trying to tell you?

Suddenly Katai turns and runs after the other Olmetecans. Before you can leap to your feet, she has vanished in the thick brush.

Turn to page 69.

"Kutewa," the boy says.

"I don't understand," you start to say. But the boy smiles.

"I speak your language," he says. "My uncle is teaching me. He is shaman of the Olmeteca—and I'm Tomi. Will you visit our village?" You've found the Olmetecans—or they've found you!

You thank Tomi and walk with him a long way through the woods. Finally you reach a clearing glowing with campfires. Tomi leads you past many thatched huts to the largest hut of all. A tall, slender man wearing a robe of bright feathers appears in the doorway. "Welcome," he says. "I am Oloac, shaman of the Olmeteca."

Oloac gives you and Tomi bowls of hot soup. You tell him about Eloisa's expedition and how you escaped from the kidnappers. "You were brave to escape," Oloac says. "Yet it would have been more dangerous to look for the Temple. There are many traps in Eagle Mountain."

"Maybe we can show you the mountain tomorrow," Tomi says. "After all, it's the greatest treasure we have."

"Tomi!" Oloac booms. His voice grows cold and sharp. "You know you're forbidden to enter the Temple until you join the medicine clan! Would you dive into the gorge before you can swim? You plunge into danger and dishonor the Sun who protects you."

Turn to page 40.

"I'd rather stay and see more of the village," you tell Tomi. "I don't want to make Oloac angry."

"Well, I'm going anyway," Tomi says. "I'll show him I'm not afraid!" Tomi turns and sets off through the woods toward Eagle Mountain.

You start back toward the village, wondering what to do. But there's no time to decide. Just as you reach the edge of the village Oloac waves to you from his hut and walks over to you. "Where's Tomi?" he asks.

When you look up at him, you feel you can only tell the truth. "He went to the Temple," you say.

Oloac frowns, but he looks more worried than angry. "Then he's in great danger," Oloac says. "He doesn't know the traps that protect the sacred mountain. I've got to stop him. I may need your help. Will you come with me?"

"Of course," you say.

Turn to page 46.

"I'll wait here for Orlando," you say, "but if the poncho is a cloak of protection, you should take it with you."

"Thanks," Eloisa says. "But if it really *does* give protection, I'd rather know you're safe." Before you can change her mind, Eloisa packs up, hugs you, and starts down the path into the woods.

You look around the tiny cabin. A loom stands in one corner. Newly woven ponchos are piled near it on the floor. In another corner a pot of soup is simmering on the stove. You haven't eaten in hours, and you can't resist tasting it. It's so good you finish the rest. The soup makes you drowsy. You lie down on the soft ponchos, and soon you're fast asleep.

When you wake up you find yourself looking up into the friendly eyes of the oldest man you've ever seen. "Welcome," he says. "I am Orlando. And *you* are sleeping on my ponchos." You sit up, suddenly wide awake.

"Eloisa should have waited," Orlando says. "She'll find a false opening into the mountain. It leads to a cursed chamber."

"How do you know all this?" you ask.

"The same way I know you ate all my soup." Orlando laughs. Then his smile fades. He looks out of the window and speaks as if to himself. "There are many secrets I haven't told," he says. "Perhaps now it's time."

Orlando turns and looks into your eyes. "I know Eagle Mountain well," he says, "for the Olmetecans are my people."

Turn to page 47.

You creep out of the cabin and run into the woods. Suddenly you hear shouts behind you. "Hey! Wake up! The kid's escaping!"

Thorny branches tear your clothes as you race away from the cabin. Then you hear shots!

Luckily the bullets glance off the trees behind you, and when you arrive in Cholula the sun is just rising. People are doing chores. They rush from their houses and surround you. "Señor Diaz! Señor!" they call.

A tall man in a suit steps out of Diego's house and runs to you. "I'm Roberto Diaz, Federal Police," he says, pulling out his badge. "Diego's father found him tied up and radioed us. You were brave—and lucky—to escape."

"They still have Eloisa tied up in Orlando's cabin," you say. "They're going to make her lead them to the Temple of the Sun. They may have already left for Eagle Mountain!"

Roberto turns to the villagers around him. "Three of you go to Orlando's cabin. You four"— he points at four men—"come with me to Eagle Mountain."

"I want to go too," you say. But the long night without food or sleep has tired you out. Your arms and legs ache from being tied so long and from racing through the woods. As you start to follow the men, your legs feel wobbly. Then everything goes black.

Turn to page 6.

Tomi stares at the floor and clenches his fists. The silence grows heavier, until you can't stand it. "Eloisa's still in danger," you tell Oloac. "Can you help me get back to Cholula?"

At first Oloac scowls at you. Then his frown gives way to a smile. "Stay with us for a time and we'll find a way," he says.

The next morning Tomi shows you around the village. Men and women stop their weaving and cooking to show you their work. After lunch Tomi takes you to the top of a ridge. He points to a huge mountain in the distance. "That's Eagle Mountain," Tomi says. "Do you want to see the Temple?"

"Sure," you answer. "But Oloac said that it's forbidden until you join the medicine clan."

"I can't wait until then!" Tomi says. "Besides, I've already heard which secret passages lead to the Temple. We can get there and back before dark."

You'd like to go, but Oloac's warning is still strong in your mind.

If you go to the Temple with Tomi,
turn to page 31.

If you say you'd rather see more of the village,
turn to page 36.

You decide not to break the shutters. There's no telling what Ramon and Juan might do if they caught you. Their voices grow louder in the next room. Suddenly Juan unlocks the door and flings it open. His gun is aimed right at you!

"Don't make a sound," he warns you. Ramon steps toward you with a potato sack and a long rope. It looks as if he's going to tie you up—for good!

"Wait!" you cry. "I—I'll tell you where the Temple is." A slow, crooked smile stretches out from under Juan's mustache. "Where is it?" he says. "Talk!"

"It's on Eagle Mountain," you tell them.

"Then take us there," Ramon says. "Let's go!"

Soon you're wedged between Juan and Ramon in a battered jeep. Ramon drives for hours over a rutted road. Finally you see Eagle Mountain. The barren summit is shaped like the head of an eagle.

Ramon parks at the base of the mountain, yanks you out of the jeep, and gives you a shove. Where can you take them?

You start forward in the direction Ramon pushed you—straight up the steep slope. You climb up to a flat table of land. Ahead of you, the mountain rises sharply up to the summit. Your heart sinks. Now you're farther than ever from help.

"We've climbed far enough," Juan snaps. He pulls out his gun and puts it to your head. "Is this some kind of trick?" he demands.

Turn to page 101.

Your heart is racing as you slowly creep across the cabin floor to where the men are sleeping. The old floorboards creak as you go. The fat man grumbles, yawns, and turns on his side. His gun lies half-hidden under his pillow. You hold your breath as you slowly bend down and reach for the pistol.

Suddenly the man's eyes blink open. He's seen you!

You snatch the gun, but the man grabs your wrist. A sharp pain shoots up your arm as he twists your hand backward and tries to pry your fingers open. You kick wildly at him, but he leaps to his feet and knocks you to the ground.

You fall to the floor, still fighting to hold onto the gun.

Suddenly there's a terrible explosion. The gun's gone off! Somewhere, far away, you hear the muffled sound of Eloisa's cry. Or is it your cry?

You don't have to wonder for very long—the bullet went in your direction.

The End

"Let's try the east face," you say. Eloisa nods and follows you down through the valley.

As you climb up the rocky mountainside you step carefully among loose boulders. The slope becomes steeper and harder to climb. Just as you think the caves will be too high to reach, you see a huge opening beyond a ledge above you. "Look!" you say, climbing onto the ledge. Eloisa scrambles up after you and peers into the cave.

Suddenly a high screech pierces the air—and a huge eagle swoops past you.

"Look out!" you cry. You cling to the rocky slope as the eagle circles and dives again. Its sharp talons rake across your back. The impact knocks you hard against the mountainside. You gasp for breath and nearly lose your hold on the steep slope.

Then, as suddenly as it attacked, the eagle soars into the sky and circles high above you.

Then you notice two eagle feathers lying near you. You pick them up gingerly and stick them into the weave of your poncho. But when you look around the ledge, Eloisa is gone! Did she duck into the cave to escape the eagle's attack?

Go on to the next page.

You pull out your flashlight and take a few steps into the damp cave. "Eloisa!" you call. An echo is your only answer.

Then, just ahead, you see footprints. Your stomach tightens into a knot. They were made by more than one person—and one set of prints is too large to be Eloisa's!

Who else could be in the cave? Why didn't they answer you? Eloisa was hiding from treasure hunters—could they have followed you this far? The thought makes you shudder, and your heart begins to pound. Have they kidnapped Eloisa? If she's in trouble, you've got to find her. But you hesitate to search the cave. In its dark passages you'd stand no chance against an ambush.

If you keep looking for Eloisa and follow the footprints, turn to page 71.

If you retrace your steps to the cave entrance, turn to page 62.

In a few minutes you're hiking with Oloac through the woods to Eagle Mountain. You follow Tomi's trail to the base of the huge mountain. From there the faint prints lead to a small opening in the mountain face.

Oloac's forehead knots with worry. "I was afraid of this," he says. "Tomi took the first opening he found in the mountain. This one leads to a deadly trap—a cavern full of poisonous snakes! I brought snakebite medicine with me, and I can scare the snakes away with a torch, but the passage is too small for me. There's a larger passage that leads into the cavern, but we'll have to walk a long way around the mountain to reach it." Oloac hesitates in front of the opening and then turns to his right. "We'd better hurry, then," he says. "We may be too late to help Tomi."

Could *you* save Tomi? You're small enough to crawl into the cave. You shudder at the thought of crawling into a cavern full of snakes, but it may be Tomi's only chance.

If you say you'll crawl into the passage to save Tomi, turn to page 74.

If you follow Oloac to the larger passage, turn to page 97.

"How can you be Olmetecan?" you ask. "I thought they disappeared long ago."

"The Olmeteca have lived in these mountains for hundreds of years," Orlando tells you. "It's only I who became lost. When I was a boy I was apprenticed to our shaman. In order to become a shaman I had to journey alone in the wilderness. On the third day of my journey I was caught in a terrible storm. Fierce winds hurled me through the air like a twig. A man from Cholula found me and nursed me back to health. I knew then that it was the will of the Sun God that I must live with the Mexicans in Cholula.

"Now I'm dying. I may have only hours left in this world. My only wish is to join my ancestors in the spirit world. For this to happen, the shaman of my people must make a sacred offering to the Sun God and pray for me. But I'm too weak to journey back to my village. If the offering isn't made, I will wander forever in the world of lost spirits."

"But how will your shaman know to make the offering if you don't return to your tribe?" you ask Orlando.

"I will tell you how you can help Eloisa if you will hear how you may help me," Orlando says.

Turn to page 117.

"Let's try the western mesa," you say.

Together you and Eloisa cross the valley below and start up the western face. An hour or so later you're hot and tired, but you've reached the flat table of land. The mesa stretches out from the base of a sheer cliff that rises up to the summit. Your hopes sink as you look among the fallen stones at the base of the cliff. You see no signs of the Temple.

Suddenly all your muscles tense. Just a few feet away you see a huge, hairy, blue tarantula. It scuttles over a white slab buried among the gray stones and disappears into a crevice in the rocks farther on. As you look again at the strange white stone, you can hardly believe your eyes. Strange marks are carved into the slab.

Go on to the next page.

"Eloisa!" you cry. "I've found something!" Eloisa rushes to your side as you uncover the long, flat stone.

"Amazing!" she cries. "You've found an Olmetecan tablet!"

"If only we could read the writing," you say. "Maybe it could lead us to the Temple."

Eloisa's face brightens. "But *we can* read it!" she says. "I've studied the writings carved on Olmetecan altars and made a translation key."

Eloisa takes a notebook out from her knapsack and sits down with you to decode the tablet:

> *Honor the Sun God, Omoteo*
> *and you may reach the sacred Temple.*
> *But if you seek to steal its treasures*
> *You'll never see the Sun again.*

"The bottom lines are too worn away," Eloisa says. "I can't read them."

For some reason you glance at your poncho. The marks around its border now look strangely familiar. Could this also be Olmetecan writing? You grab Eloisa's notebook and search its pages.

"I've found the missing lines!" you cry. "They were woven into the poncho all the time!"

Turn to page 76.

You start out of the cabin and find the path marked by the red thread on Orlando's map. You grope through the dense brush, following the signs woven into the map. First you pass a tree bent like an arch. Then you find a boulder shaped like a head. There you also find a brook and follow it upstream.

Then you see it—the Olmetecan village! Large huts with smoke holes in their thatched roofs are nestled in a clearing by the brook. Men in leather pants and women wearing long ponchos gather at the edge of the village as you draw near. They stare at you in surprise.

A man wearing a long robe covered with feathers steps forward. "Welcome," he says, "I am Oloac, shaman of the Olmeteca. Only one other has ever chanced upon our village. He taught me your language. But I see by your poncho and bracelet that you're not here by chance."

"Orlando sent me," you answer. "He's been living with the Mexicans in Cholula. But now he's dying. He sent me to ask you to make the sacred offering for him."

"It shall be done," Oloac says. His eyes are shining with tears. "We thought Orlando had died long ago in the great storm. But you have more to tell."

Go on to the next page.

You tell Oloac about Eloisa. "Orlando said she's trapped in a cursed chamber," you say. "I've got to find her!"

"Those who stay in the chamber slowly lose their will," Oloac says. "If we reach her too late, even my medicines can't heal her."

"Isn't there another way?" you ask Oloac.

"There is, but it's even more risky—for you," Oloac says. "With the Medicine Vision I can enter a trance and speak into the minds of my people. If I knew Eloisa I could go into the trance and tell her to leave the chamber. Since I don't know her, I can only try to give you the Medicine Vision. But I must warn you: The Vision is as dangerous as it is powerful. You could save Eloisa—or you could stay in the trance forever."

If you try to warn Eloisa with the Medicine Vision, turn to page 85.

If you ask Oloac to come with you to help Eloisa, turn to page 89.

Juan and Ramon are still snoring as you creep out of the shelter into the light of the full moon. As you start up the rocky mountain, you can see the bonfire burning on a plateau high above you.

The climb would be difficult even with your hands free. One false step now, and there'll be no way to break your fall. Just as you think you can't climb any farther, you find a narrow ledge that leads across the cliff beneath the plateau. On the other side of the cliff the mountain slopes up more gently. It looks like the only way to reach the plateau.

Your heart's racing as you inch across the ledge to the other side of the cliff. From there you soon make your way up to the plateau. Beyond the trees ahead you can see the blazing fire. You draw closer and look between the branches.

You can hardly believe your eyes. Indians are sitting around the fire! Their long black hair is braided with bright strings of beads, and they all hold long knives. Everyone wears ponchos except for two women sitting across from each other, who wear skirts of feathers. One woman's body is painted with red stripes.

You watch the Indians for a long time. No one says a word. Then, as if by some secret signal, the two women sitting across from each other stand up. The woman painted wih red stripes walks around to the second woman and presses a knife to her heart.

Turn to page 106.

54

You stay hidden in the bushes. As the sun rises over the eastern mountains, the Olmetecans begin to sing. The song is so strange and beautiful that you don't hear the twig snap in back of you.

Suddenly you're grabbed from behind. It's Juan and Ramon! "We'll teach you to run off!" Ramon shouts.

The Olmetecans stop singing. "They've heard you!" Juan snaps. "You *always* blow our cover! Let's get out of here. Grab the kid!"

You kick at Ramon as he lifts you onto his back and tries to run from the clearing. The Olmetecans leap to their feet. Juan faces them and shoots his gun in the air. "Stand back and no one will get hurt!" he shouts. The Olmetecans freeze at the sound of shots but then press forward again. They seem unafraid.

"I warned you!" Juan shouts. He's shooting at them!

Turn to page 66.

You hurry along the path through the woods marked by the blue thread on your map. If you can find Eloisa soon enough, maybe you can still help Orlando. You hike all morning across ridges and valleys until you reach a tall mountain shaped like an eagle with outstretched wings. You've reached Eagle Mountain!

On your map the thread leads to a huge tree and then turns left—straight into the mountain. Just ahead you see a huge tree near the base of the mountain. You walk to the tree and search the rocky slope. As your eyes adjust to the shade you notice a small opening—a tunnel!

You take the flashlight out of your pack, turn it on, and step into the damp passage. Did Eloisa pass this way? You can't see any footprints on the sheer rock floor. You continue on deeper and deeper into the heart of Eagle Mountain. Suddenly a wall blocks your path. It's a dead end! Could Orlando's map be wrong?

Then you notice deep crevices cut into the wall. They look like hand-and-footholds. You look up and see a small hole above you. It's filled with light! Climbing up the wall is almost as simple as climbing a ladder. You climb easily through the hole.

Turn to page 58.

You start up the slope ahead of you, heading straight back to Cholula—you hope. You bushwack through some brambles, then clamber up a long rocky slope. Pine saplings are growing through tiny crevices in the rock. You grab them to steady yourself, praying that they won't give way.

It's slow going, but you finally reach the top of the slope and climb down the other side. You try to keep heading in a straight line away from the stream, but you have to cut back and forth over the rocky terrain in order to cross each new ridge. As you struggle to the top of each ridge your hopes begin to fade. By cutting straight across the ridges you should get back sooner than if you retraced the way you came when you escaped from Juan and Ramon; you should have reached the village by now. But you've been hiking for over an hour without finding any trace of Cholula.

You sit down on a flat rock at the top of a ridge, wondering what to do. Should you stay where you are and hope someone will find you? Your stomach tightens into a knot. Who would be looking for you besides Juan and Ramon? Does anyone even know you were kidnapped?

You feel as stranded as if you were on a deserted island. But as the minutes pass, you start to imagine that you're being watched.

You turn around, searching the trees and shrubs on all sides. Suddenly someone laughs above you. You look up. An Indian boy is perched on a limb above you! He drops to the ground.

Turn to page 34.

"I'll join the temple builders," you say.

The chief builder bows her head. "I am Ulama," she says. "You will have a good home in my hut."

The next day Ulama begins to show you how to cut different kinds of stone. After you've been working all morning, your first stone shatters into a million pieces. "Our work takes great patience," Ulama says. "To judge well, one must see all the flaws in a stone as well as the veins of gold."

"When do we work in the Temple of the Sun?" you ask Ulama. "What are its mysteries?"

"I can't tell you in a word, just as you can't carve this stone with one blow," Ulama says. "When you have carved a panel of the shaman's lodge, we will take you to Eagle Mountain."

It's hard to wait until you can go to Eagle Mountain, but the builders are friendly. They tell ancient stories and sing songs while they work. Each day you grow more used to your new life. You work hard and soon learn how to carve every kind of stone. In fact, you soon forget about getting back to Cholula.

One day, Ulama is watching you carve a jaguar into a panel of the shaman's lodge. "You're ready to work in the temples on Eagle Mountain."

"Temples?" you say. "I thought there was just one—the Temple of the Sun."

Ulama smiles. "The Temple of the Sun is the oldest and most sacred temple," she tells you. "But there are more places and secrets in Eagle Mountain than you have dreamed of. And soon you will know them."

The End

58

You've found the cursed chamber! Huge stone statues line the walls. Some have human bodies but the wings and beaks of fierce birds. And Eloisa is there! She's standing at the far end of the room with her back to you. She seems hypnotized by the largest statue of all. It has the body of an eagle and the head of a snake.

"Eloisa!" you call. Eloisa turns to you as if she's asleep. What's wrong with her?

"We've got to get out of here!" you say. "This isn't the Temple. Orlando said this chamber is cursed!"

Eloisa stares at you as if she's watching a movie. She doesn't resist as you take her by the hand, lead her to the ladder, and tell her to climb down. You're about to follow when a thought stops you. Why not take some of the treasure?

If you climb down and lead Eloisa out of the mountain, turn to page 88.

If you stop to take some of the jewels first, turn to page 90.

At first you pound the shutters as lightly and quietly as you can. But they're nailed tight.

"Quiet in there! Stop what you're doing!" Ramon shouts from the next room. They've heard you! Quickly you grip the stool and swing it as hard as you can against the shutters. The wood breaks away with a loud crash and clatters to the ground.

"Stop where you are!" Juan shouts. He fumbles at the locked door and bursts into the room—just as you squeeze through the window.

You drop to the ground, scramble up the hill, and duck between the slats of a high fence. As you run into the forest, you look behind you. Ramon is rounding the side of the house. He's running up the hill after you. It's lucky he's too fat to squeeze through the fence! You run deep into the thick woods, cutting back and forth across ridges and hills until you're sure Ramon has lost your trail.

You stop to rest by a bubbling stream and wade into the cool water, splashing water on your face until you begin to feel better.

The sun is getting low in the west. You should be heading back to Cholula. But as you look around, you're not sure which way to go. You made so many turns that it might be hard to retrace your steps in the fading light. Maybe you should head up the steep slope in front of you and try to head straight back to Cholula—if it's the right direction.

If you try to head straight in the general direction of Cholula, turn to page 56.

If you try to retrace the winding way you came, turn to page 29.

What treasures can you take with you? You reach into the pool of gold, but the water is deeper than it looks. You can't reach the gold at the bottom.

Do you dare take the crystal eagle? Your heart is racing as you lift the statue. It's much heavier than you imagined, and you stagger under its weight as you turn toward the passage. The sharp crystal facets cut into your arms. Then, as you reach the small opening to the passage, you almost fall beneath the eagle. The ground is shaking. It's an earthquake! You put down the statue and crouch on the ground as the earthquake gets stronger. You've got to get out of here!

You plunge into the dark passage. It's like trying to crawl on the deck of a storm-tossed boat. Stones rain down on you like hail, and dust chokes the passage until you can hardly breathe.

When the earthquake is over, you're bruised and shaken. The passage widens as you press on, but it seems to go on forever. Have you taken a wrong turn?

The thought stops you short. The main passage seemed bigger to you than the other passageways. But now the passages you cross seem bigger than the one you're in.

You wander for hours, desperately looking for a way out of the maze of stairways. As the beam of your flashlight flickers and dims, your hopes of finding the way out grow just as faint.

The End

62

You step outside and walk along the ledge, keeping careful watch on the eagle still circling overhead. Suddenly you hear a man's voice behind you. "Freeze!" he shouts. "One false move and we'll throw your aunt over the cliff!"

Slowly you turn and face a tall man with a bushy mustache. He's holding Eloisa's arms behind her back. Another man—this one hugely fat—grabs you and pulls you to the edge of the cliff.

"This is your last chance, Eloisa!" the fat man shouts. "Where's the Temple?"

"Wait!" Eloisa cries. "I'll tell you." The fat man smiles and pulls you away from the cliff.

What can Eloisa tell them? Is she stalling for time? "It's the poncho," Eloisa says. "It's a—"

"SKREEE! SKREEE! SKREEE!"

An eagle's cry splits the air. It's attacking! The two men drop you and Eloisa and shield their faces with their arms as the great bird dives down.

Your poncho protected you before, but what about Eloisa? You scramble across the ledge, cover her with the poncho, and brace yourself for the eagle's attack.

But the blow never comes. With a deafening screech the eagle dives at the tall man. It knocks him against the rocky ledge, rises, and attacks the fat man. Soon they're both out cold. The eagle rises high in the air, circles three times, and disappears in the sun's glare.

Eloisa grabs the men's guns. "They'll be up and walking soon—right into prison," she says.

Turn to page 3.

As you turn and scramble down the rocky slope you can still hear Juan and Ramon calling to each other. "Look at these jewels," Juan cries. "They're priceless!"

You reach the jeep and jump behind the wheel. You turn on the motor and start to pull away. Suddenly, the whole jeep is lurching and rumbling. You're losing control! You slam on the brakes and turn the engine off, but the jeep keeps shaking. Then you realize—it's another earthquake!

The earth thunders as it shudders and heaves. Then you hear a sound like gunfire. Are Juan and Ramon shooting at you? If they catch you now there's no telling what they'll do!

But the cracks aren't gunshots. They're the sound of huge boulders breaking away from the summit of Eagle Mountain. It's another avalanche!

You cling to the ground as the plateau above you shudders beneath tons of falling rock. It's crushing the pyramid! The mountain is swallowing up the strange chamber it uncovered—along with Juan and Ramon!

When the earthquake quiets and the ground is still, you start the jeep and turn toward Cholula. When you reach the village you're still trembling. You'll never forget your narrow escape.

The End

When you wake up, you find yourself lying on a straw mat in the middle of a small thatched hut. Your poncho is spread over you, and a woman is kneeling by your side. She smiles at you and offers you spoonfuls of warm soup. "I am Tamana," she says. "The Sun led you here just in time!"

"Where am I?" you ask.

"We are the Olmeteca," Tamana answers. "We call this place Shelter of Omoteo, for everything here is protected by the Sun God, Omoteo."

A shiver runs down your spine. You've found the Olmetecans!

In the next few days Tamana brings you soup and sits with you as you slowly become stronger. One day she points to your poncho. "We don't know how you found this poncho," she says, "but you have worn the sacred symbols of our people. The sun, the eagle, and the mountain spirits protect us. Yet you kept the pattern hidden. That is why you became lost. Our shaman, Oloac, has said you must come before him. Then we will know if you will join us and honor the spirits that protect us. If not, you must leave us and never seek to return."

"When do I meet the shaman?" you ask.

"Now," Tamana answers, picking up your poncho. "He's waiting for you."

Turn to page 108.

A woman falls, clutching her leg. Then, with a long, wailing cry, the Olmetecans throw their knives. Ramon wheels around just in time to see Juan fall. Another knife whistles through the air. Ramon throws you down and races toward the steps, but the knife is faster. It strikes him square in the back.

You're thrown clear of the knives—but with your hands tied behind you, you can't break your fall. You crash through a bush so fast you hardly feel your head hit the rock underneath.

The Olmetecans bury your body in the sacred Temple of the Sun. "This spirit died too soon," their shaman says. "But may it soon find the path to the Sun." The tribe holds a great feast to give you strength on your journey to the spirit world.

The End

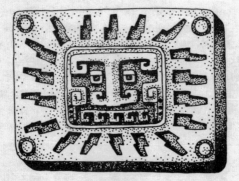

The two men push you into an old jeep and speed through the town to a rutted road leading into the mountains. They drive for over an hour until they reach a barren, deserted mountain ridge. On the crest of the ridge you see a tiny shack. The fat man shoves you through the dusty shack and into a back room. There's another door but no windows in the bare room.

"We won't lock you in," the fat man says, opening the second door. Outside there's nothing but air!

"A landslide took away all the ground between this room and the cliff," he says. "Tell us where to find your aunt or we'll let you go—right out this door! You've got five minutes to think about it."

The two men slam the door. You're alone.

You peer out of the doorway. The jagged rocks drop sharply away below. You could never climb all the way down to the bottom of the cliff. Then you notice a narrow ledge about ten feet below the door. It runs along the cliff to a gentler slope on the right. There, a grove of pine trees covers the slope. If only you could reach their cover!

Do you dare try to reach the ledge? One loose rock could send you to the bottom of the cliff. Even if you made it to the slope you'd still be far from Cholula. If you tell the men where Eloisa is you might find a better chance to escape.

If you try to climb down to the ledge, turn to page 24.

If you tell the men that Eloisa is hiding in Orlando's cabin, turn to page 26.

Oloac sighs and shakes his head. "We were too late," he says. "Her memory is lost forever. Only with years of care and powerful medicines can I wake her from this trance. But even then she'll have to learn everything again like a baby—even how to talk."

"Will you do it?" you ask. "We can't just let her die!"

"Because of what you did for Orlando I will help your aunt," Oloac says.

He puts his hand on your shoulder. "But you must return to your people," he says. "Eloisa must leave behind her old life in order to break the curse. We shall not meet again."

A year later you explore the rocky ridges near Eagle Mountain. But you can't find any trace of the Olmetecan village. Even the passage leading to the cursed chamber is nowhere to be found.

Did Eloisa survive the curse? Would she know you if she saw you? It looks as if you'll never have the chance to find out.

The End

You search the brush where Katai left the clearing. Not even a broken branch marks the Olmetecans' trail.

You search the whole plateau, but there's no sign of the Olmetecans. There's nothing to do but start back down the mountain slope. At least with your arms free the going is much easier. It's good to know you can make it back to Cholula.

Soon you reach the ledge that crosses the cliff below the plateau. As you start to edge around a huge rock, a sudden, strange feeling stops you short. You touch the amulet at your neck—and your fingers tingle. A faint buzzing sounds in your ears. Then you hear voices! You hold your breath and listen.

There are people on the ledge ahead! You inch forward and peer around the outcropping. Ramon and Juan are walking toward you. They've seen you!

Juan lunges forward to grab you. You dart back behind the rock and hug the cliff face desperately. Juan clutches at thin air. He's lost his balance! He twists in the air and grabs Ramon's arm to steady himself. But Ramon struggles to shake his arm free and keep his own footing. Then, with a scream, Juan pulls Ramon down with him, hurtling to the base of Eagle Mountain.

You cling to the cliff face until you stop shaking. Finally you make your way slowly down the mountain. You find the jeep at the campsite with the keys still in the ignition. You start the motor and head back to Cholula.

Turn to page 81.

You follow the footprints farther into the cave. "Eloisa!" you call. "Are you there?" This time not even an echo answers. Suddenly you slip on the mud and loose stones. You're falling faster and faster—not down the steep passage, but through the ground as it collapses beneath you!

When you wake it's pitch dark. You try to stand up. Then you realize that you *are* standing—half-buried in mud and stones. You try to dig your way out but soon grow tired and faint.

Go on to the next page.

In the dark, silent cave you can't tell how many hours are passing. Just as you're about to give up hope, you glimpse a faint gray light coming from behind you. You strain to look over your shoulder. There you see a dim triangle of light. As it brightens to a rosy yellow, you realize that you're looking through an opening in the cave. The sun is rising!

With new hope you dig again at the mud and stones that trap you. Finally you free your legs and start to crawl out of the cave. Then you cry out in horror.

It's light enough in the cave to look around you now. And you see that you're crawling over human bones!

Turn to page 113.

You hand the bowl of blood back to Oloac. "I can't join your people," you say. "I'll have to find a way home soon."

Oloac frowns and looks into your eyes. "You have spoken with your heart," he says. "But if you cannot honor our spirits, you must leave us now." Oloac clasps his hands, and suddenly a fire flares up from the ground before him. Tamana takes your poncho from you and holds the poncho over the flames.

"O Sun, protect us," she calls. "We return this weaving to you." Tamana lays the poncho over the flames. Your heart sinks as the beautiful weaving bursts into flame.

"The Sun led you here," Oloac says. "Though you turn away from the Sun's will, we pray that the Sun will be merciful and lead you home."

As you slowly wander away from the Olmetecan village you wonder about the shaman's words. Will you ever find your way to Cholula?

Turn to page 86.

"Wait," you tell Oloac. "I'll crawl into the passage to save Tomi."

Oloac swings around. His face brightens. "You are very brave," he says. "I fear it's our only hope."

Oloac lights a torch and gives you a clay flask. "Keep the snakes away with the torch and give Tomi the medicine in this flask as soon as you find him," Oloac says. "Stay with him until I come through the larger passage."

You scramble over rough slabs of rock and cold stretches of mud. Your eyes smart from the smoke of your torch. "Tomi!" you call. "Are you there?"

There's no answer. Then you hear a sharp rattling. A rattlesnake is blocking the passage!

You clench your teeth and thrust your torch at the angry snake. The snake slithers back, hissing and rattling. But just ahead, you hear a noise that makes your stomach twist into a knot—the sound of not one but dozens of rattlers. You press forward until your passage opens into a large chamber.

At the sight before you, you break into a cold sweat. The chamber floor is covered with rattlers! Tomi is lying unconscious in a corner just a few feet away. And dozens of snakes are crawling over his body.

Turn to page 110.

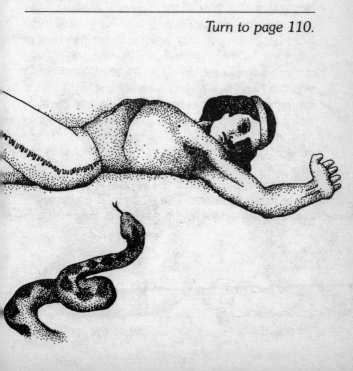

With Eloisa's help you quickly read the message on the poncho. You find the same lines carved in the tablet and then read:

We build a stairway to the Temple.
We climb winding stairs to the Sun.
The ways are many, the paths are steep
That pass through darkness to golden light.

"You've found the clue!" Eloisa says. "We should look for a stairway that leads to the Temple!"

"We'd better start looking, then," you say, and begin to search the cliff for signs of a stairway. After an hour you stop to rest in the shade of a huge boulder. Your eyes ache from searching so long in the sun's blinding glare.

For a while you can hardly see at all. Your vision is patchy and your head is throbbing. You take a long drink from your canteen and stare at the cliffs before you. Then, slowly, your headache fades and you can begin to make out fissures and outcroppings in the cliffs that you couldn't see in the sun.

"I've found it!" you cry. Half-hidden in shadow is a narrow staircase. The steps lead as far up as you can see—right to the summit of Eagle Mountain.

Go on to the next page.

Eloisa rushes to your side. "The Temple must be at the very peak of the mountain," she says.

"Let's find out," you answer, starting up the steps. Soon you reach a narrow ledge with a dark shadow to your left. It's an opening in the cliff! You take the flashlight out of your pack and shine it into the opening. More steps lead down into the cave.

"The poncho said that the stairway leads to the sun," Eloisa says. "Can there be two stairways?"

One stairway leads right up the cliffs. It looks like a dangerous climb. The inner staircase looks easier, but the stairs go down instead of up.

Which way should you try?

If you follow the stairs leading down into the mountain, turn to page 83.

If you climb straight up the mountain, turn to page 118.

Somehow you manage to choke down the bowl of blood. The Olmetecans burst into song. The singing grows louder and louder—until Oloac raises his left hand and the room falls silent. Oloac raises his face to the sun and chants:

"One was lost, now one is found,
The Sun sets and rises.
The Sun God shines upon your life
Among the Olmeteca."

Tamana steps forward and puts your poncho on you with the right side out. "Now you may truly wear the symbols of our people," she says.

"Thank you," you say. But the ceremony is not over. Oloac claps his hands again. A man and a woman step into the circle of light and stand on either side of you. The man who stands on your left wears a leather vest painted with jaguars. He carries a bow and a long fishing spear. The woman on your right wears a vest sewn with beads of jade, silver, and gold. She places a leather hide on the ground and spreads upon it many carving tools. Their sharp edges glisten in the sun.

Go on to the next page.

"Now, before the spirits that protect us, you must choose your path," Oloac says. "On your left you see our best hunter. He knows all the ways of the woods. When we are not growing corn the hunters feed and clothe us. On your right you see our chief temple builder. The temple builders make our homes and guard the mysteries of the Temple."

The hunter is tall and muscular. He seems ready to sprint up a mountain. The chief builder bears herself with wisdom and calm. You feel you could happily follow either path. But once you make the choice, will you give up your chance to find your way back to Cholula? Now that you have bound yourself to the tribe, do you dare ask to leave?

Tamana touches your shoulder. "Do what is in your heart," she says. "Whether you choose to become a hunter or a temple builder, we are all your brothers and sisters."

If you join the hunters, turn to page 93.

If you join the temple builders, turn to page 57.

If you say you just want to go back to Cholula, turn to page 94.

You wonder what made you stop on the cliff. Your whole body still tingles. Did the amulet warn you?

When you arrive in Cholula, people surround the jeep. A woman with curly gray hair runs forward. It's Eloisa! "I'm so glad you're safe!" she cries.

When you tell Eloisa your story she shakes her head. "I'm afraid you've had a terrifying visit," she says. "But I wish I'd been with you. You've seen the Olmeteca tribe!"

You show Eloisa your amulet, and she studies it for a long time. Then she looks up at you, with shining eyes. "Katai gave you a magic talisman," she says. "It's made to protect the wearer. Since it kept you from running straight into Juan and Ramon, I'd say it's only begun to prove its worth."

The End

82

You climb over broken earth and rubble to reach the burial chamber. Through the opening you can hear Ramon and Juan laughing. "Everything's made of silver!" Ramon cries. "And this coffin—it's covered with rubies and pearls. They'll be worth millions in the United States!"

You step slowly into the dim chamber. Juan and Ramon are shining their flashlights on a silver coffin in the center of the chamber. They're so busy filling their knapsacks with jewels that they don't even see you enter.

Then an amazing sight stops you short. One wall is covered with an eagle-mountain pattern like the one on your poncho. But a shiver runs down your spine as you see that the sun is black instead of gold. The chamber is filled with beautiful treasures, but the black sun hangs above you like a terrible warning.

"Let's open the coffin," Ramon says. "Think what treasures will be buried inside it!"

"Think of the *skeleton* buried inside it!" Juan answered.

"Are you afraid?" Ramon shouts. "Then I'll do it!"

Turn to page 98.

"Let's try the stairs leading down into the mountain," you say.

They lead down through a long, low passage. After a few minutes the steps turn to the left. Farther on they level out and spiral up to the right.

You're glad that you're not scaling the cliffs, but the passage soon makes you feel uneasy. It turns, leads down, and rises so much that you lose all sense of direction. Soon you're not even sure if you've climbed farther up toward the summit or down below the mesa. From time to time you cross other passageways leading off in other directions. "By sticking to the main passage I think we can keep from getting lost," you tell Eloisa.

"I think so too," Eloisa says. "But this passage seems to be getting smaller. I wonder if it's really the main passage."

Eloisa has to bend over to keep from hitting her head and soon you're both crawling on your hands and knees. Finally Eloisa stops. "I can't go on," she says. Though it's cool in the cave, her face is sweaty and red. "The passage is too small for me. I've got to get some air. I'll wait for you at the entrance to the cave."

You continue along the shrinking passage. Suddenly a flat slab of stone blocks your way. You push against the slab with all your strength. It won't budge. Then, just as you're about to give up, the great slab shifts to your right. When you try to slide the slab sideways, it moves easily into a crevice in the wall.

The sight before you is worth all your work.

Turn to page 107.

You hesitate to leave your only defense against the rattlers, but Oloac is already retracing his steps. You lay the torch down and follow him through the chamber. The torch sputters—it's going out! You grab hold of Oloac's robe, shuddering. The snakes' rattling sounds angrier than ever, but they don't strike.

You wind your way out of the chamber, through a long, dark, passage, and outside again to the slope of the mountain. Oloac lays Tomi down in the shade of a tree and puts a muddy-looking cream on his snakebites. Then he turns to you.

"Tomi will need to sleep for many days, but you saved him in time," he tells you. "Thank you."

"But how did you walk into the chamber without getting bitten?" you ask. "I could hardly keep the snakes away with my torch until you came."

"The members of the medicine clan have many powers that seem strange to you," Oloac says. "Many of your people only want to steal our sacred land. But you didn't try to rob the Temple. Instead you risked your life to save Tomi. Your act was worthy of a shaman."

Oloac takes a necklace of eagle talons from his belt and puts it around your neck.

"This is a circle of healing," he tells you. "Wear it and sickness will run from you like a mouse from the eagle. We have hidden the ways to our village, but you will always find us as easily as the eagle flies to its nest. Together let's look for your aunt and take her to our village for a feast in your honor."

The End

Oloac leads you through the village to a small stone building. You follow him into a dark room and watch as he builds a fire to prepare for the Medicine Vision. He sprinkles a blue powder onto the flames, and smoke with the smell of pine fills the room. Then Oloac takes a root from a pouch at his belt. He puts it in a bowl, grinds it into powder with a smooth rock, pours the powder into a bowl of tea, and gives it to you to drink.

You drink the tea while Oloac begins to chant:

> *"Only a fool will stare at the sun.*
> *But look into this fire,*
> *See there the Medicine Vision:*
> *Seek truth and it will not blind."*

As the smoke thickens, your head begins to feel light. The flames before you swirl around and around like a whirlpool, pulling you in.

In the swirling flames you begin to see a shadowy figure. It's Eloisa! She's surrounded by great urns of jewels, beaded robes, and masks of gold. She stares at the glittering treasures with blank eyes. It's as if she's in some kind of trance.

"Eloisa!" you call. "Leave the chamber! There's a curse on it!"

Eloisa stirs, but then falls back into the trance. "Hurry!" you say. "Get away before it's too late!" Eloisa staggers backward and slowly turns toward a hole in the floor. As Eloisa begins to climb down through the hole, the golden treasures dissolve in the crackling flames before you.

Turn to page 111.

Days pass with no sign of any village. Finally you can't go on. You lie on a bed of soft moss, shivering with cold. You're more hungry than you've ever been. Everything looks blurry. The tree above you sways in the breeze. It looks like Tamana.

Could it really be she? Tamana moves toward you, reaching out to touch your shoulder. "Tamana," you call. "Help me!"

"Wake up. Can you hear me?" she says.

"Yes—I couldn't find my way back!" you say. But Tamana doesn't seem to hear you. She shakes your shoulder. "Wake up, we're here to help you!" she says. But the voice is different now—it's deep and husky. Tamana's figure fades, and in her place you see a circle of blurry faces hovering over you. The faces spin around and around until you shut your eyes against the dizzying sight.

"I'm afraid we're too late," the husky voice says. "The poor kid's delirious after so many days of exposure."

Hands lift you up onto a stretcher and cover you with blankets. But you feel as if you're buried under blankets of snow. As the search team carries you back to Cholula, you begin to feel numb.

Even if you survive the trip to Cholula, your chances are slim. In these remote mountains there's just no way to get you to a hospital in time.

The End

You turn away from the treasures, climb down the wall, and lead Eloisa quickly down the passage. Soon you're standing under the huge tree at the base of Eagle Mountain.

"I . . . I feel so strange," Eloisa says, rubbing her forehead. "What happened?" Then, slowly, she begins to remember. "You saved my life!"

When Eloisa can think again you tell her how you found her. Eloisa's face grows pale. "I'll go back to be with Orlando," she says. "I only hope you can find the Olmetecan village in time." You say good-bye to Eloisa. At least now she's safe.

But when you look at the map Orlando gave you, it's changed. The colored threads have run together! The map is blurred into a vague purple shape. There's no way you can use it.

You wander around Eagle Mountain for hours, looking for some way to find the Olmetecan village. Finally you turn and walk slowly back to Orlando's cabin. The journey seems to last forever. When at last you reach Orlando's cabin Eloisa meets you at the door.

"Orlando passed away," she says. "Perhaps he didn't know it until the end, but he made his own sacred offering. He told you how to find me as well as his tribe. Then he gave you his armband. He said it is a Medicine Band made for him by his grandfather. To give it away is a great sign of trust among his people. Before he died he said to tell you: 'You've chosen well. Be at peace on your journey. Your path is just beginning. Now I follow mine to the mountains of the Sun.'"

The End

"Will you come with me to Eagle Mountain?" you ask Oloac. "I can't help Eloisa if I stay in the trance forever."

"I'll do what I can," Oloac says.

Even though Oloac leads you quickly along hidden paths, the sun is already low in the west by the time you reach Eagle Mountain. Oloac leads you to a cave at the base of a high cliff. He lights a torch, steps inside, and leads you down a narrow passage.

Soon you reach a stone door and Oloac pushes it forward. Nothing could prepare you for the sight before you. Eloisa is standing frozen as a statue. She's surrounded by huge stone statues, half-animal and half-human.

"Eloisa!" you say. Eloisa doesn't move at all. What's happened to her? And what's happening to you? A strange, sweet smell is invading the chamber. It makes you feel tired and dizzy. You've got to get out of here!

You hold your breath, take Eloisa's cold, limp hand, and lead her out of the chamber. Oloac follows you down the passage in silence.

When you are outside again you shudder at the sight of Eloisa's pale, lifeless face. "Oloac!" you say. "Can't you do something?"

Turn to page 68.

The room is so filled with riches that you hesitate, wondering what to take. Next to the hole you climbed through is a huge urn filled with pearls and turquoise. To the right of the urn is a silver statue of a hawk. You step toward it, but then something else catches your eye—the golden eagle with the serpent's head.

Your heart is pounding. It's the statue Eloisa was staring at! The serpent glows with a strange fiery light. Are you dreaming? The chamber was dark and cold when you came in. Now it feels warm and bright. The golden serpent seems to sway back and forth. Suddenly you're dizzy. What's happening to you?

Just then, Eloisa is at your side, tugging your sleeve. "You've got to break away," she says. "There's something deadly about this chamber!"

Eloisa's words seem to come from far away. It's as if she's at the end of a long tunnel. Even though she's standing beside you her voice grows fainter and fainter.

Shouldn't you be scared? Your pulse was racing before. Now your heartbeat is so slow you can't feel it at all. It doesn't matter. Nothing seems to matter. You take fewer and fewer breaths now. It doesn't seem as if you need to breathe. And it's not long before you stop breathing altogether.

The End

"When the Spanish invaded Mexico, many Olmetecans fought to the death. But their great shaman, Toloc, promised to lead his people to a place where they could still live in peace. Only a hundred survived the journey to these mountains. When they reached Eagle Mountain they built the Temple of the Sun in thanksgiving for their new home.

"Toloc prayed day and night to the Sun God: 'Grant me the power to protect my people forever from invaders and I will sacrifice my life.'

"The Sun God answered Toloc's prayers and gave him the power to start and stop the earth's shaking. Toloc went to Eagle Mountain and carved this secret in the Temple walls.

"But Toloc had to keep his promise—to sacrifice his life for his people. When he returned to the village, a lightning bolt struck Toloc down! But the Sun God wasn't finished.

"From the shaman's ashes three eagles rose into the air. One eagle forever guards the Temple. The second protects our village. The third is the spirit of Toloc. Every generation his spirit is reborn in the next shaman. Toloc lives in me: Oloac, shaman of the Olmeteca!

"You are the first who has not tried to steal the Temple's treasures. You give us hope that not everyone in your nation still seeks to conquer."

Oloac turns and opens the door he came through. "But now we must go," he says. "Eloisa has worried about you long enough."

The End

"I'll join the hunters," you say. At your words the chief hunter puts his hand on your shoulder. "I am Adu," he says. "May your spears fly straight and far with ours."

Adu gives you a pair of the leather pants worn by all the hunters. He shows you how to spear fish, shoot with a bow and arrow, and set snares with looped vines. Soon you can creep through dense brush silently and whistle like the forest birds.

"Every hunter has a special bird name," Adu tells you. "I am called Night Owl because I like to hunt at night."

But it's Adu who wakes you the next morning before sunrise. Drums are beating in the square outside. What's happening? "Come," Adu says. "It's time for your naming!"

When you reach the square no one is in sight. But the hunters' birdcalls sound all around you— and suddenly hunters leap from behind every hut, dancing wildly around you and waving a cloak of feathers.

The dancers lift you up, throw you high into the air, and catch you in the feather cloak. Over and over you soar through the air.

Finally the Olmetecans put you down. Adu steps toward you with a long cloak of silvery feathers. "Now you know what it is to soar like a bird. Know all the beasts as well, for you are one of them." Adu puts the cloak around you and turns to the rising sun. "You will be called Falcon," he says. "For you are swift to move and quick to learn. You will see far and soar to great heights."

The End

"I want to go back to Cholula," you say. "I can't join the tribe."

A deadly silence fills the room. The shaman stares deep into your eyes. "You may want to change your mind," he says, "but you cannot break the bond of blood." The shaman chants strange words and blows a red powder over you. It's getting hard to breathe!

What's he doing to you? You begin to feel dizzy and sick. "By the power of the Sun God I name you Toloc, wandering spirit."

The shaman claps his hands three times, and the Olmetecans turn their backs to you. "Go from here!" the shaman says. "But you will wander, never united with any people!"

Suddenly the sun shines directly through the opening overhead. You cry out and shut your eyes to the blinding glare. The sun seems to burn through your clothes. Then you feel as light as a leaf blowing in the wind. You're floating!

You can't think. The shaman's words ring in your ears: "It's the Sun that decides your fate. You will drift with the clouds and wander in the streams!"

A strange spell has taken hold of you! You're rising through the opening in the chamber, high into the air. You try to cry out, but you've lost your voice. You sound like the wind rustling the leaves below. You rise higher and higher until you sail among the clouds. Then you realize it—you *are* a cloud!

Turn to page 102.

Tomi turns toward the setting sun and bows his head. Then he climbs down into the crevice and holds up his bow. "I give up my bow in thanks to the Sun God," he says. "I'll wait to join the medicine clan before I seek the Temple again."

Tomi lowers his bow and fits it between the rocks that trapped Eloisa. Then he waits in the crevice and looks up at you.

"What offering will you make to the Sun God?" he asks.

What can you leave behind? You climb back down into the crevice and look up at Eloisa. Can you give up your poncho? Eloisa nods as you lift your poncho over your head. "We give up this poncho in thanks to the Sun God," you say. You put the poncho next to Tomi's bow and climb out of the crevice.

"We shouldn't have come here, but now at least we've honored the Sun with our offerings," Tomi says.

Suddenly you smell smoke. "Look!" Eloisa cries. "The poncho is smoldering!" You step toward the crevice, but Tomi grabs your arm and pulls you back.

All at once, the poncho bursts into flames. Blue snakes of fire leap up along the length of Tomi's bow. Then a still more amazing thing happens. In the leaping flames and thick, swirling smoke you see Oloac's figure spreading a cloak of flaming feathers.

"Behold and honor the Sun God!" Oloac cries. "Your gifts will unfold greater mysteries than the ones you sought to steal."

Turn to page 15.

You take one last look at the Temple. The points of sunlight on the ceiling sparkle as brightly as the golden pool and crystal statue. Finally you take a deep breath, turn from the chamber, and start down the winding passage.

As the passage gets bigger, you grow worried. The passage is thick with dust, and stones are scattered on the floor. Suddenly the ground begins to tremble again. It feels as if you're in a tunnel with an oncoming train. You press on, but the heaving earth keeps throwing you against the rough walls. Finally the stairs lead up again. You see light ahead—and Eloisa is waiting at the opening of the cave!

"Hurry!" she cries. "Avalanches are starting all over the mountain!"

You sprint up the last stairs. With Eloisa you hurry down to the base of the cliff and race to the middle of the plateau. When you finally stop and look back, thick clouds of dust are rising from the cave. It's caving in!

Eloisa turns to you. "Thank heavens you came back in time. But did you find the Temple?"

You tell Eloisa what you saw. Her face brightens—and then a look of sadness crosses her face. "The passage is sealed and the cliffs are too steep to climb," she says. "I'm afraid you're not only the first but also the last outsider to see the Temple of the Sun."

The End

You have to run to keep up with Oloac as he hurries across the steep mountain slope. His forehead is furrowed and his face is pale. "I hope we can find the passage in time," you say. Oloac doesn't answer. He only walks faster.

Finally you clamber over some steep rocks and climb up to a broad ledge. There you find a cave in the mountainside. It's big enough for Oloac to enter without bending over. You're about to follow when he turns and holds up his hand.

"Wait here," he snaps. "If you get bitten, I can't carry you both out."

Before you can answer, Oloac turns and disappears into the dark cave. You wait on the ledge, watching the sun sink lower and lower in the west.

Finally Oloac steps out from the cave. He's carrying Tomi in his arms—but the boy's face is as gray as stone. He lies very still in Oloac's arms.

Oloac's voice trembles as he speaks. "We were too late," he whispers. "I did all I could. If you will be our friend, warn Eloisa to stop searching for the Temple. She knows even less than Tomi about the Temple and the ways to honor the Sun God."

A knot tightens in your throat. "I could have crawled into the first passage," you say. "I might have reached Tomi in time!"

Tears well up in Oloac's eyes. "We all think of the paths we did not take," he says.

Oloac looks into your eyes. "Tomi will never learn the sacred paths to the Temple," he says. "But you still have many paths to choose from. May you choose a path that leads to the Sun."

The End

Before Juan can answer, Ramon runs to the coffin. As he raises the heavy lid you glimpse the sparkling jewels and golden bowls inside.

Suddenly a blinding light flashes from the coffin and a bitter smoke fills the room. "Arghhh!" Ramon screams. He drops the lid and falls to his knees, covering his eyes with his hands. You've got to get out of here!

Then you hear a terrible crash behind you. You swing around, but it's too late—a flat stone slab is blocking the entrance. You're sealed in!

You slowly turn and face Juan and Ramon. Ramon is still kneeling and covering his eyes. "It was booby-trapped!" Juan shouts at Ramon. "We're done for!"

You look around for another way out of the chamber, but there's not even a crack in the smooth walls and ceiling. The dusty air is already growing thin and stale.

Juan turns to you, seeing you for the first time among the treasures. It looks as if you'll be sharing the most beautiful tomb in the world.

The End

As you walk around the room, you see that the carvings on the walls are covered with pearls. When you look again at the ceiling, the pattern seems strangely familiar. It's a map of the stars!

On one side of the ceiling you see a large hole that looks like the moon. The pale light shining through the hole is growing brighter. As the sun moves across the sky it shines upon different parts of the ceiling. Now the sun is shining directly through the holes on the west side of the dome.

Suddenly a bright shaft of light shines through the moon hole, lighting the gold like a blazing fire. The crystal statue flashes like a thousand tiny mirrors. Then, in the dazzling light, you see a circle cut into the wall below the statue.

Your heart is racing as you press against the circle. It moves forward! You push the slab several feet into the rock. When you stop pressing the slab, it rolls by itself into a niche in the passage.

You shine your flashlight into the chamber before you, unable to believe your eyes. The floor is covered with green jade and blue turquoise arranged to look like a huge map of the world.

You step into the chamber and look up. The domed ceiling sparkles with countless silver beads. This star map shows the Milky Way and the dense star spirals of other galaxies. Below the dome the circular wall is covered with Olmetecan writing. If only you had Eloisa's notebook!

Turn to page 105.

What will you do now? You begin to tremble.

"You sure got the kid scared," Ramon tells Juan. But you're not shaking with fear—the whole mountain is trembling beneath you! Ramon staggers forward, trying to keep his balance. "It's an earthquake!" he cries.

Suddenly the earth heaves and splits. You fall to your knees and cling to the ground. It seems as if the earthquake will never stop. Then, above the quake, you hear a deafening roar. The slope ahead is crashing down! It's like a waterfall of earth and rock.

Finally the mountain is still. You look through clouds of settling dust to the broken cliffs—and you can hardly believe your eyes. The earthquake has uncovered part of a pyramid! A round opening is cut into its base.

"It's really there!" Ramon cries. Together Juan and Ramon clamber over the rubble and stand at the entrance of the pyramid. "It's a burial chamber," Juan cries. "We're rich!"

Juan and Ramon seem to have forgotten about you. You'd love to see what's inside the pyramid, but could you look in and still get away?

If you follow Juan and Ramon into the pyramid, turn to page 82.

If you run back down the mountain right away, turn to page 64.

As night approaches and the air cools, it begins to rain. You find yourself falling with the rain into a wide stream. The bubbling stream carries you far into the mountains. You race over steep rocks and swirl in the eddies of deep pools.

Where will the stream take you? You can already tell it will be a restless journey.

The End

"Now we're getting close," Juan shouts. He grabs the shovel from you and digs furiously. Then his shovel cracks against a clay urn. "I've found it!" he cries. "It's mine, all mine!"

Ramon's face turns pale. "Juan," he says, "we're partners, right? We split everything fifty-fifty."

"I'm in charge!" Juan shouts. "You'd still be looking for junk in the dump if it weren't for me."

"The sun is making you crazy," Ramon says. "Either we split the treasure or no one gets a thing!"

As Juan and Ramon begin to fight they seem to forget you're there. You step back from the pit and edge toward the path down the mountainside. You can still hear them shouting as you turn and scramble down the mountain. Halfway down the rocky slope you hear gunshots.

Are they shooting at each other or at you? You don't wait to find out.

The sudden blow of a bullet in your back stops you short—then sends you tumbling down the slope.

The End

Could there be more secret doors hidden in the patterns? There are! You find three more doors like the one you came through, placed at the points of the compass around the map.

Then you hear the sound of grating stone. A shiver runs up your spine. The door across from you is opening!

You hold your breath as a tall man steps into the chamber. He's wearing a long robe of beautiful feathers.

"Don't be afraid," the man says. "You've come far and found much that is secret. It's an honor even for Olmetecans to come to the Inner Temple, but since the Sun God has shown you here, you may learn something of its purpose. Then I will show you another way out. The Temple is safe from earthquakes, but the passage you came through will soon cave in. Your aunt will grieve for you until you return."

"How do you know all this?" you ask. "Do you mean that the Olmetecans are still alive? What's happened to them?"

"In one breath you ask to know the past, the present, and the mystery of who I am," the old man says. "But all things are woven together like the threads of your poncho. The mystery of who I am is woven into the present, and the present is woven into the past."

You listen as the man continues.

Turn to page 91.

You hold your breath as the painted woman cuts the other woman's skin, drawing blood in long red stripes like the ones painted on her own body.

The bleeding woman looks ghastly pale, even from where you watch. But she doesn't cry out or struggle, and although she sways, she doesn't fall. Then she begins to chant. Others join in, and soon the chanting sounds as strong as the beating of drums:

"Omotec. Teo-teo. Olmeteca."

Olmeteca! A shiver runs up your spine. These must be the people who built the Temple of the Sun!

When the chanting slows and the bleeding woman sits down again, the sky is growing rosy in the east. Where did the time go? Juan and Ramon will soon know that you've escaped. You've found the Olmetecans, but can they help you?

You want to have your hands free as soon as possible. The trip back to Cholula would be long and dangerous with your hands tied and kidnappers on your trail. On the other hand, the ceremony was bloody: Would the Olmetecans really free you?

If you show yourself to the Olmetecans, turn to page 33.

If you stay hidden and watch further, turn to page 54.

You're staring into a chamber glowing with light. As you step into the chamber, you see that the sun is shining through tiny holes in the domed ceiling. It's like looking up at a starry sky. You're at the very peak of the mountain—right inside the eagle's crest. You've found the Temple of the Sun!

The walls are carved with strange figures—half-animal and half-human. The floor is covered with silver tiles. At one end is a pool of sparkling water. When you look into the pool, you see why the water is sparkling: Its bottom is covered with gold!

Then you notice the most amazing treasure of all. Set into a niche above the pool is a statue of an eagle made of solid crystal. Its eyes are sparkling diamonds.

Suddenly the ground trembles beneath you. Just as suddenly, the tremor is over.

Your throat tightens into a knot. If a stronger earthquake blocks the passage, this may be your last chance to see the Temple—or to escape from it.

Should you go back? Should you try to take anything back with you? People might not believe you've found the Temple without proof. On the other hand, the writing on your poncho warned against stealing from the Temple.

If you leave without taking any treasure, turn to page 96.

If you take some of the treasure with you, turn to page 61.

If you explore the Temple further, turn to page 100.

You follow Tamana out of the hut into the bright morning sunshine. Her hut is one of many that surround a large square. In the center of the square is a round stone building. "This is the shaman's lodge," Tamana tells you. "Once you go inside you must do only what is in your heart."

You enter the building nervously. The shaman is standing in a dazzling circle of light that shines through an opening in the ceiling. He wears a golden mask with an eagle's beak. Men wearing capes of colorful feathers stand pointing their long spears toward him.

Tamana motions for you to kneel in the circle of light. The shaman towers above you. He begins to chant. Then he claps his hands, and a boy steps forward bearing two clay bowls. Oloac sprinkles you with liquid from each bowl. One of the liquids is water—the other, blood. The shaman drinks deeply from both bowls and offers them to you.

"Water is the life of our tribe," he says. "Blood is what makes us one. Drink from both bowls if you honor the spirits that protect us. You will always be bound to us and we to you."

You drink from the bowl of water and then look around you. The room is silent. Everyone is watching you.

You want to be friends with the Olmetecans, and you're thankful that they saved your life. But you hate the thought of drinking blood.

If you drink the bowl of blood, turn to page 78.

If you say you'd rather find your way home, turn to page 73.

110

Frantically you wave the torch at the snakes in front of you, trying to herd them away from Tomi. Finally you reach his side.

Tomi doesn't seem to recognize you. He's burning with fever and trembling with chills. His legs are swollen and red. "Oloac!" he cries. "Help me!"

"Drink this medicine," you say, putting the flask to his lips. "Oloac is on his way." Tomi sputters and coughs but manages to drink the medicine. Slowly he falls into a deep sleep. You feel more awake than you've ever been as you stand guard with your torch. Finally a light appears at the far end of the chamber. Oloac's coming!

To your horror, he walks right into the chamber of snakes! You start to cry out, but Oloac raises his finger to his lips. His eyebrows are drawn together and his eyes are half-closed. It's almost as if he's feeling his way, step by step, among the snakes. Yet instead of rattling in anger, the snakes lie quietly on the ground. Why aren't they biting him?

When Oloac reaches you he lifts Tomi into his arms and turns back the way he came. "Follow me," he whispers, "and leave the torch behind!"

Turn to page 84.

You wake from the Vision feeling tired and feverish. Oloac presses a cool cloth to your forehead. Then, as you look around, you see that you're back in Orlando's cabin.

"How did we get here?" you ask Oloac.

"I carried you here," Oloac says, "and Eloisa is on her way. I sent a helper to lead her here. She won't remember what happened to her. But because you saved her in time she'll remember everything else about herself—and you."

"Where's Orlando?" you ask.

"Two of my helpers have already carried him back to our village," Oloac says. "Because of your Vision I reached Orlando in time to give him my medicines. You truly have the Medicine Vision within you. Use it well."

"But how do I use it?" you ask.

Oloac smiles. "I can't tell you how to use your Vision," he says. "You may not be able to speak into others' minds again. But if you look deeply into the flames, your Vision will give you strength. Those with the Vision become our greatest artists and leaders."

Oloac takes a ring from his finger and hands it to you. In its center is a golden sun.

"This ring is worn only by those with the Medicine Vision," Oloac says. "Wear it to remember us and the strength within you. It is a gift from the Sun God." Oloac slips out the door.

You stare at the ring he gave you. It's a wonderful gift. But the best gift of all is the sound of Eloisa at the door calling your name.

The End

You turn and sprint up the hill, ducking under branches and scrambling over jagged rocks. But the man is catching up with you. "Stop, or it'll be worse for you later!" he shouts. "Ahh! Ow! These branches!" he cries.

The man can run faster than you, but you can slip more easily through the dense brush. You veer to the right, where the hill is overgrown with thickets and trees. It's your only chance to escape him. Thorns scrape your arms and legs as you duck into the brush, plunge headlong through the thicket, and race up a long steep ridge through the shelter of vines and low branches. Behind you the strange man's curses sound farther away and fainter. You look back and almost laugh out loud. He's tripping over vines and hopelessly caught in the tangled branches.

But you should have been looking ahead as you run over the crest of the ridge. Right in your path there's a pile of loose rocks; and beyond that, nothing—just thin air and the long drop down to the bottom of a cliff.

What a terrible end to your trip! At least they won't get your map—whoever *they* are.

The End

Suddenly a huge figure steps through the cave opening—an Indian.

He's wearing rough leather pants. His brown chest is painted with yellow stripes, and he wears a necklace of bird talons. He holds a huge ax in one hand and grabs your arm with the other. You feel too weak to resist. He pulls you out of the cave and raises his ax, ready to strike.

Then he freezes and his jaw drops open. His eyes are fixed upon the feathers still clinging to your poncho.

High above you, two eagles screech and circle in the air. The man throws away his ax and drops to his knees. The eagles dive down and land by your side. Their cries fill you with a strange energy. What's happening to you?

Your whole body begins to tingle. Suddenly the rising sun flares brighter than at midday and thunder splits the clear sky.

Then the feathers on your poncho begin to grow. They grow longer and broader until they become great wings. Your legs shorten and become powerful talons. Your eyesight becomes so sharp that you can see a rabbit running in the valley far below. When the eagles fly into the air, you beat your wings and soar up after them, hovering on the wind currents lifting you high above Eagle Mountain.

Turn to page 115.

As the years pass, you hear the Olmetecans telling their children your story. They tell how Tilok the hunter was guarding the cave of the dead when he saw a human rise from the bones and turn into an eagle before his very eyes. The Olmetecans point to you from below and call you Petoc, mountain spirit. Their words float up to you

like the smoke from their fires—small signals in the vast sky.

Among the clouds and cliffs of Eagle Mountain you have found an even greater mystery than their words can tell.

The End

Orlando reaches into the folds of his cloak and holds out a small piece of weaving. "Here's a map of Eagle Mountain," he says. "If you follow the black threads, you will find my village. The white threads on the map will lead you to Eloisa. In a vision I saw her trapped in the cursed chamber. You can still find her and warn her in time."

"But how can I choose between helping you and my aunt?" you ask.

"I hope that you can do both tasks," Orlando says. He takes a gold armband from his cloak and puts it on your arm. "Wear this," he says. "It was given to me before I made my first journey. It will give you strength, whatever you do."

"How can I take your gift?" you say. "I haven't even *decided* what to do!"

"You don't have to tell me your choice," Orlando says. "At times we must all journey alone."

Orlando hobbles to a chair by the stove. His face is as gray as ashes. He sits down and closes his eyes, leaving you alone to make up your mind.

If you try to find the Olmetecans first, turn to page 50.

If you try to find Eloisa first, turn to page 55.

"Let's climb up the outside of the mountain," you say. "We may reach the summit sooner this way."

It's like climbing a ladder that's five stories high. Your arms and legs begin to ache, but there are no more ledges where you can sit and rest. Suddenly a step gives way beneath your feet!

Desperately you cling to the steps with your hands. Eloisa ducks to avoid the falling rubble. She climbs toward you, trying to help you find a foothold. She's too late. The rock you're hanging from gives way. You're falling!

You won't be one of the few to return from Eagle Mountain. As you plummet through the air, you can only hope that Eloisa will be luckier than you.

The End

ABOUT THE AUTHOR

ANDREA PACKARD graduated from Swarthmore College in 1985, where she studied English and Art History. *Secret of the Sun God* grew out of her experiences during two summers in Mexico. Her first book, *The Evil Wizard*, was published in 1984 as part of Bantam's Skylark Choose Your Own Adventure series. Ms. Packard is currently studying painting at the Pennsylvania Academy of the Fine Arts in Philadelphia. She continues to write and illustrate stories for children.

ABOUT THE ILLUSTRATOR

YEE CHEA LIN is a graduate of Cooper Union in New York State. In addition to *Secret of the Sun God,* he has illustrated many other books for major publishers. Mr. Lin is currently at work creating the artwork for an upcoming Choose Your Own Adventure book.

Coming in July